I0445268

THE
CRYSTAL
INN

THE CRYSTAL INN

A Southern Haunting

Jennifer Donner

Copyright © 2022 by Summerland LLC

All Rights Reserved.

This novel is fiction, except for the parts that aren't.

This book is dedicated to all of the spirits that helped me write it.

TABLE OF CONTENTS

CHAPTER I

The Inn was an eerie place in a small town in North Carolina. I drove by a lot, always wondering what it was... seeing it set far back from the two-lane, kudzu-covered, weeping willow tree-lined road – in the small village.

I had heard rumors that it used to be a grand restaurant and that not much had gone on in about ten years or so.

Many of the seemingly abandoned estates in Glowing Rock used to be summer resorts for the wealthy, but that was back in the 1950s and '60s.

The Inn hadn't struck me as odd or piqued my interest & my curiosity hadn't ever taken me much further up the winding driveway to the dark, somewhat run-down building. I just assumed it was another failed business since the economic downturn.

That is, until one day I had seen an advertisement for employment. It was a simple ad; all it said was "Hiring Innkeeper. Apply in Person."

I had spent my first few years after college in the South, waiting tables and running up my debt more than I could handle. I thought this job might be the perfect opportunity since I had grown up in an inn & it paid more than double what I was making at Mable's.

Monday morning, I put on a nice dress and a pair of shiny black heels. I fixed my hair into a low ponytail and drove over – up the long winding driveway, past the deteriorating lamp posts.

It was the end of summer then, and I remember the grass was nearly half as tall as my compact car, making the Inn feel even more secluded from the already small village.

I pulled in & around the circular driveway to the *almost* empty parking lot in the back of the building, with the exception of one older black Cadillac.

Eerie was my first thought. *Haunted* was my next.

"Perfect," I whispered to myself as I walked up the side of the building and around to the Mansion.

The vast front porch was lined with sets of wrought iron chairs that had mismatched cushions & a wrought iron dining table sat on the far right. Spider webs hung from various dark corners & draped from Charleston-style gas lanterns.

Not only was I a horror movie fanatic, but as an aspiring writer, I thought it would be the perfect material. I would have taken the job for a mere $3 an hour just for some fresh ideas.

If I had known just how much material I would actually get, I may have turned right back around, got in my car, and gone back to waiting tables... writing about horribly demanding customers and oversized apple pancakes.

After carefully walking up the creaky steps of the porch, trying not to trip in my three-inch wedge heels, I entered through a weighty & towering door – into the lobby.

(As a waitress at several breakfast places, I was used to sneakers. During the summer – I wore sandals or tennis shoes on my off days, so three-inch black business heels were difficult to walk in.)

Entering into the foyer was like stepping back into time even more. A grand Persian rug covered almost all of the dark brown hardwood floor. Intricate wallpaper that was beginning to peel and curl at the corners lined the walls that led up to the tall ceiling & a glistening antique chandelier hung from the center of the room.

There was no one around, so I sat down on a vintage brown leather couch, and clutched my (somewhat deteriorating) brown writing notebook that doubled as a makeshift briefcase. The sweat on my hands was starting to cause tiny marks on the faux brown leather as my nerves began to rise.

I had been sitting out in the lobby for what seemed like eternity – but it was only about 10 minutes, in reality.

I better ace this interview if I ever want to be a real bonafide writer, I thought. Well, that, and get my family off my back for my "lack of drive," they would say. If I heard one more comment from a stuffy aunt in Connecticut about how I was wasting my life away waiting tables, I was going to have a mental breakdown.

Soon I heard slow shuffling steps down an adjacent corridor.

"Hello?" I inquired, in a low whisper.

I've always been kind of soft-spoken, but I was extra nervous because I really wanted the job, so my tone was quieter than usual.

"I'm here for the innkeeper job," I said, as a petite man appeared from around the corner.

He invited me into his office, a small dark room off the lobby with a view of the front porch & only a glimmer of sunlight coming through the picture window to the outside.

From the office, you could see the sprawling field that rolled down past the front of the Mansion. A vast front lawn that hadn't been mowed the entire summer, I assumed.

"Tell me about yourself," the man began.

It was awkward, so very awkward. I didn't know what to say. (My usual demeanor at most job interviews.) I did know, however, that I shouldn't begin by telling him that I'd spent the past few years waiting tables and hiking – "wasting my degree," as my family would say. So, I mumbled on about how I grew up in hospitality and had a business degree. I mentioned how my parents had built an inn and that growing up, I'd done everything from housekeeping to inn-keeping.

After listening to me ramble on about random topics for about ten minutes, he stopped me mid-sentence by putting up his hand and staring at me from behind his tired brown eyes and small brown face.

"You're hired, be here at 9 am tomorrow," he said, in an accent I couldn't really put my finger on.

He hadn't even glanced at my resume, even though he had been holding it in his small, wrinkled hands, for the entire interview. Still, I was so elated I had been hired I didn't bother to think twice about how strange that was.

I couldn't believe it! I practically ran to my car and sped home like a race car driver so that I could get on the phone with every living relative and friend I had worked with within the past few years to proclaim my enthusiasm for my new career.

I'm a real working woman! I thought, later that night as I was making dinner. Not to mention – this place was haunted. I knew it was haunted. I just had that feeling when I walked up. It was like stepping into a real-life haunted house, except this place was like a mansion. Ok, it wasn't 'like' a mansion. It *was* a mansion.

CHAPTER 2

The next day, I decided to take the back way to work. Driving through the old roads that led to the heart of the village, past several ancient cemeteries that must have been over 100 years old (at least), which totally added to the creep factor.

I arrived at the Inn at 9 am sharp and entered the lobby again to find Mr. Crystal sitting in one of the blue wingback chairs – across from the brown leather sofa I had met him sitting at the day before.

He told me that he didn't "want me stealing" and that if I broke anything, to "notify him immediately" he then said he was "off" and that the "files were at the front desk."

That was it.

No training.

No guidance.

He also snuck in a quick comment that he "didn't want to be my friend."

I was a bit horrified that there was no formal training, but anything was better than toiling away for measly tips at a breakfast restaurant, wanting to throw syrup at the next customer who complained that their coffee was too weak.

Not to mention – by taking this new job, my pay had almost doubled.

I'm a real working woman... I'm a real working woman, I kept reminding myself.

When Mr. Crystal had said "files," he wasn't kidding. There were brown files, boxes of files, files with files, file holders with files, plastic containers with files. I didn't know where to start.

To be honest, I wasn't even sure what my job description was, let alone which file to start with. And the worst part was, I was alone – so if I had a question or someone wanted to book a room, there was no one to ask for help. I didn't even know what the nightly rate was!

Mr. Crystal had literally disappeared. I wasn't sure where he even went, but I *was* sure I didn't have any way to get in contact with him since he always left his phone on the desk in the dark office adjacent to the foyer.

About two hours into the workday, I got my first phone call – it was Sophia, Mr. Crystal's wife.

She had a similar accent but much softer and sweet.

"Corrine!" she proclaimed when I picked up the phone. "I wanted to help you with training. I won't be in until tomorrow to show you the bookkeeping, but if you could, take the keys and go through every room to familiarize yourself. Make sure each room has two shampoos, soaps, and four for the suites. We have guests coming in soon for the holiday weekend. And make sure you lock them on your way out."

Phew, I thought. *This should give me about a week to prepare for the guests.* But soon I began to panic again. *What if we get more guests? What if someone walks through the door? I've had no training whatsoever!*

I grabbed the two large, round, heavy key rings, that were hanging off hooks on the wall behind the check-in desk & began my self-guided tour of the Inn. The key rings held (at least) multiple keys for each room, all mis-matched in color and shape. There was one for the first floor, one for the second, and one for the third floor.

Every room was different – and marvelous they were. But dusty. It looked like people hadn't stayed there in months, perhaps even years. *And why hadn't I seen a housekeeper?* I wondered.

The Crystal Inn had twenty rooms. The inn I'd grown up in had 28 rooms, and we always had multiple housekeepers – daily. The lack of staff struck me as peculiar, but I just grabbed a duster and lightly cleaned the rooms while taking note of all the old photographs and an-tiques, cataloging them in my mind so I could hopefully use them in a story later.

After checking the toiletries and dusting, I carefully locked each room behind me, heed-ing Sophia's instructions.

Another thing that struck me as odd was that I was told to keep all of the lights off. The only lights to be kept on were two small lamps in the main lobby, a couple in the office, and a few in the bar and restaurant area.

It was silent. Dark and silent.

– Except for me opening and closing and locking each creaky, heavy door.

At the end of my first day, I got a call from Cherri, the previous innkeeper who had been fired on account of a heavy drinking problem and stealing a jar of spices (or so I was told by Mr. Crystal).

Cherri was now working at another smaller inn in a nearby town. I hadn't had many phone calls, so I was elated when the phone actually *did* ring.

"Have you been up to the third floor?" Cherri asked when calling about her last paycheck.

"Yes, why?" I replied, thinking she must be joking.

"Well, it's haunted."

"Come again?" I asked.

"It's haunted. There are ghosts up there. Just be careful, sweetie."

Click.

"I'm a horror fanatic, but this woman is flat-out crazy..." I whispered to myself after Cherri hung up.

...

Later that night, I called my friend John, who was the baker and cook at my last job – thinking he might know the inside scoop about the Inn. He was a local and had a bunch of other local friends in construction that I assumed must have known the area well.

"You're working where?!" John shouted in his loud, burly, southern voice.

"The Crystal Inn," I repeated.

"The Crystal Inn?!"

"Yes, John, the Crystal Inn," I repeated again, with a slight crack in my voice this time.

"Oh boy. Yup. Had some friends that did some work up there a few years back. Said they heard voices on the third floor of kids playing. Thing is – my friends, the guys, were the only ones in the Inn, well them and Old Man Crystal. Rumor has it he's got some fortune buried out at some castle in France. Don't know why he don't fix that place up and mow the lawn. Don't know why he changed the name, too. Glowing Rock Inn used to be a hoppin' place back in the day when my parents were young. Buddies of mine went out there for an estimate to fix up that roof there, and he never called 'em back."

"Voices of kids playing?"

"Yup. That's what I said. Not to mention there's some old Civil War history there. Be careful."

"Right, John, well anyway, I already miss you guys at Mable's. Save me a piece of lemon custard!"

Click.

I just chalked it up to John being a crazy local – or at least his friends were.

I mean, I thought the Inn was maybe haunted, but I hadn't heard voices of children playing – that was just plain insane.

"I'm a working woman," I repeated to myself again, put on some comfy sweatpants, and went to bed early so I could be well-rested for my second day on the job.

...

That next day I met the groundskeeper, Andres. He was a Hispanic guy from Florida who didn't talk much but had a friendly demeanor and smiled a lot. He asked me for a key and said hello. I had seen him trimming hedges, on my first day at the Inn.

I only saw Mr. Crystal for about five minutes, that morning – when I first arrived to work. He had grabbed a tattered old hat with a tennis ball and two racquets embroidered on the front of it and shuffled down the hallway, mysteriously disappearing until the end of the day, yet again.

Based on the tennis racquet mounted over one of the two fireplaces in the bar, plus the trophies that were lined up on the mantel below – I imagined Mr. Crystal might have been quite the tennis player in his heyday.

That afternoon, I decided to walk around outside the Mansion and found not only the grass, but everything to be overgrown. Again, from growing up at an inn, I knew it was nearly impossible for Andres to maintain the entire grounds of such a vast estate all alone.

I saw pictures of the gazebo in a photo album behind the front desk wedged between the "files of files." Couples wearing ivory wedding gowns and black tuxedos were happily posing under the pristine alabaster structure, which was now overgrown with weeds and kudzu.

The tennis court now had a giant tree growing out of the middle of it. Large patches of forest green & ivory paint were chipping off the side of the Inn & the metal bench that sat outside near an empty birdbath had begun to tarnish and rust.

The large room that housed the bar and breakfast area was grand, ornate, and kept up – unlike the rest of the Inn. It had a copper tiled ceiling that must have been twenty feet high with an intricate design pressed into it, an extensive collection of old-fashioned-looking wooden tables, and a grandiose fireplace that made you feel like you were at one of the Vanderbilt estates.

The almost always lifeless, yet pristine, kitchen – was the only other room that wasn't covered in dust.

...

Not long after my walk outside and around the grounds, two couples from Alabama stopped by and asked if they could see a room before they committed to staying. Since we had been pretty much dead the day before, I exclaimed, "Gladly!" and showed them up to a suite on the second floor.

As we made our way back down the grand staircase blanketed with crimson red carpet that led to the foyer, Mr. Crystal mysteriously appeared after being gone nearly all day. He was standing at the bottom of the staircase, scowling intently at us. I shot a half-worried smile at him and continued to walk the couples through the three grand dining rooms, turning on and off the lights to the many chandeliers as we went, trying to adhere to the "no light policy."

"Do you know any of the history of the Inn?" the woman with a short gray bob hairstyle asked.

"Well, no, but I heard there's quite a bit of Civil War history. I'll have to do my research...."

I ended our mini tour of the Mansion at the bar in the breakfast room and offered them some coffee or wine. They declined but thanked me for being so hospitable and asked if they could take a brochure.

"Brochures! Of course!" I exclaimed. But, when I went to the front desk to grab one, I realized we didn't have any brochures. Not even a single business card.

Minutes after the group of tourists left through the lobby, Mr. Crystal reappeared, staring at me with an angry, yet expression-less, look. It seemed like he was almost look-ing into and through my soul.

"No tours," he stated, with a hint of irritation in his voice.

"Oh well, I just assumed..."

"No tours."

And that was that. No tours.

"Well, what about brochures? I wasn't able to find any under the—."

"No brochures and no lights," Mr. Crystal bellowed, interrupting me mid-sentence and then shuffling off to some unbeknownst loca-tion.

My elation from getting a new, better-pay-ing job quickly died down – *No tours, no bro-chures, no lights, no housekeeper, and hardly any guests. What in the world would I do all day? Sift through old files of files and dust off photographs from the 1800s?*

Well, at least it was "haunted," and I'd get some good material, I thought – even though I hadn't seen (or heard for that matter) the slightest inclination of a haunting for myself.

My attitude had turned pretty grim, but my demeanor quickly changed around about 4 pm that day when Sophia showed up; she was a breath of fresh air.

Sophia was the exact opposite of Mr. Crystal.

She was dressed all sleek-like, in black head to toe, with a puffy jacket that had bold stripes of bright pink down the arms. She had long flowing brown hair and a youthful face. I guessed her age to be around forty, and she looked like she could have stepped right out of one of those fancy ski magazines that I found amongst the files under the front check-in desk.

Sophia brought me a freshly baked pastry that she mentioned she had made from scratch herself, that afternoon. It was so flaky and warm; the delightfully spiced apple filling made me drift off for a minute... Daydreaming, I pictured myself walking into a pastry shop in Paris and picking it out in person.

Granted – I had never been to Paris, let alone Europe, but the taste and smell of the apple strudel made me feel like I had.

After Sophia had shown me the bookkeeping, we got to know each other by laughing over our college days. It seemed like we had bonded. I even felt comfortable enough to ask her why in the heck there was no housekeeper.

"Well, we just don't have that many guests – just a few in the summer and then a couple of return guests that will come on select weekends in the fall."

I thought it was odd that there weren't any guests – but Sophia and I had really hit it off.

Things were looking bright.

CHAPTER 3

My third day went pretty normal until after lunch when I got a call from a lady looking for employment.

"Well, the position has been filled by, er – me, but you're more than welcome to drop off your resume..." I stammered to the woman on the other end of the phone.

"That's ok, dear; I don't even have transportation right now. I was just calling to inquire. Have you found the gold room yet?"

"No. What gold room?!" I excitedly asked.

"The gold room – it's said that one of the Civil War soldiers buried gold in room twenty-two. We used to go in there as kids. Every year when I was little, The Glowing Rock Inn used to have a big Halloween celebration. In fact, my aunt used to work there. She would let us climb down in the hole... Maybe you can shimmy down there? Rumor has it there are tunnels buried deep underground. Take a real good look at the pictures on the walls, too; they'll talk to you."

"Did you say talk to me?"

"Yes, dear, they'll talk to you. Captain B.T. Morris has his portrait up on the wall in the back hallway; he's the one that hid everything. Well, have a good afternoon, and good luck."

"Thank you. You have a good afternoon too."

I squealed with excitement as I quickly hung up the phone and rushed up to room #22, lugging the hefty set of keys for the second floor with me.

And what do you know? After moving back the small rug beside the bed, cut marks in the hardwood floors that made the shape of a small square were revealed. I pulled up the piece of wood to find a small hole that led to a much larger hole. Even with a flashlight shone into it, you couldn't see much but dirt and cold, damp darkness, (and presumably spiders). Unfortunately, there was no gold glimmering, but it was still an amazing find. It was something else to add to my future story about the haunted hotel.

Since I hadn't discovered a stack of gold bullion, my hunt was on for the portrait of B.T. Morris.

I disguised my treasure hunt as a cleaning spree (in case I ran into the somber-looking Mr. Crystal). I grabbed the scruffy duster and headed down the long corridor of the back hallway that led from the kitchen to the lobby.

The scarlet lobby walls were adorned with black and white photo after black and white photo & a few really old-looking oil paintings of men wearing fancy tailcoats, holding rifles, and riding large brown horses.

After dusting about twenty other pictures, carefully trying not to knock any down, I finally found the one with B.T. Morris, dated 1864.

"Cool!" I shouted, looking around to make sure no one had heard me, either Mr. Crystal or the "ghosts".

Turned out, Captain Morris was actually quite handsome with a stoic expression and neatly trimmed beard. I stared into the picture and studied the way his thick dark hair was combed slightly to the right and how each gold button on his uniform glistened. And then, I suddenly felt faint – very faint. I thought it might be best to walk outside to the garden area to get some fresh air. So, I took the door to my right out through the lobby and entered the gloomy and dark ballroom. I set the antique-like duster behind one of the small brown wooden chairs that lined the ballroom walls. A ballroom that I imagined was quite glamorous back in the day (when lighting was allowed).

That was when it hit me - a whiff of cigar smoke.

I knew cigar smoke.

My dad was a gambler and a cigar smoker. After he and my mother divorced, he moved to Florida and gambled away half of the small fortune he got from selling their inn in Maine.

The creepy thing about the cigar smoke was that I was the only one in the Crystal Inn at the time. Also – I knew cigar smoke well enough to know this wasn't any type of average cigar smoke; it smelled old – and musty.

"Holy Crap. Holy Crap. Holy Crap." I whispered.

I was so excited I had my first haunted moment at the Mansion; I instantly forgot that I was feeling woozy and had been headed out to the garden. I walked back to the duster, picked it up, and placed it back behind the check-in desk – deciding to take a break and admire some more of the old photographs on the walls in the lobby. It didn't hurt that some of the soldiers were quite striking.

I mean, I *was* the only human soul in the Mansion 90% of the time, and I was sick of looking at files and waiting for the phone to ring. I deserved some downtime.

Plus, the overwhelming smell of the cigar smoke was almost *too* realistic, and I was beginning to get a little spooked. So looking at pictures of handsome soldiers from the 1800s seemed to be a good idea to distract myself.

And that's when things got really weird (weirder than me ogling men from the 1800s).

The longer I stared into their eyes, the stranger and weaker I felt, almost as though I might collapse.

I decided to go into the dimly lit ladies' room and splash some water on my face to help snap me out of my daze. When I looked back up into the large mirror above the sink, the air suddenly became heavy and thick. The distressed age patches in the mirror made my surroundings seem even more blurry and foreign. I forgot where I was and who I was, for a brief moment.

The mix of emotions and sensations came on so strong; I thought I might fall onto the tile floor, so I leaned onto the countertop for some fleeting sense of stability.

The small bronze lamp with the red beaded lampshade began to flicker on and off. That was my cue to head back to the front desk and avoid any old photographs or any other room in the Mansion that was too far from my handbag and car keys.

Begrudgingly, I chalked my amnesia & light-headedness up to the leftover sushi I ate for lunch. But the scent of the cigar smoke was still looming in my head...

...

The rest of that week was pretty uneventful. I barely even saw Andres or Mr. Crystal. Sophia only came in at night after it got dark, so we kept missing each other, which was a shame. Sophia reminded me of my mom and home, with her fresh-baked pastries.

Mom always baked cookies for my high school and college friends after classes but moved to Tennessee to take care of my grandmother after she and Dad divorced, so she was a few hours away. I barely got to see her, except for a handful of weekday trips I was able to sneak in on my meager budget from working at Mable's. I thought I'd plan a longer trip soon now that I had some extra gas money.

...

The next week, we finally had guests for the holiday weekend. A few groups with children had come to Glowing Rock to go horseback riding and enjoy the long Labor Day weekend. The parents would jokingly ask about ghosts, and the children would laugh.

Everything was pretty normal and lighthearted until the new housekeeper, Maria, came down to the front desk after lunch on Saturday.

"Miss Corrine, we have a problem on the third floor," she said in a sweet tone. "Guests are complaining that their toilet is broke."

"Ok, no problem, Maria. We'll get Andres to come up and check it out."

"Ok, I don't want to be alone too..." Maria said in a softer and lower tone, sweat dripping from above her thick brows.

"What's that, Maria?" I asked.

"I don't want to be alone. My sister – she used to work here. She said it was haunted. She quit because she was too scared."

"Well, let's get Andres. We'll all go up together," I suggested.

After about twenty minutes, Maria and I found Andres outside trimming hedges. The estate property was so vast I'm surprised it didn't take two hours to find him.

Andres and I followed Maria up to the third-floor suite where the family of five was staying, the parents with their three small children.

Maria had *all* of the lights on.

"Maria, we need to keep the lights off in the areas we don't have guests, Mr. Crystal insists," I reminded her.

"No. We can't. I'm scared."

"But he insists. It's not me, Maria," I replied.

"No, if we turn the lights off – I will quit and leave. And Miss Corrine, I found this," she said, as she held up a picture of a ghost-like figure – drawn in black chalk pencil on a piece of torn white paper. The oblong shape had a face with lifeless eyes, overly long arms, and lanky hands grasping around a muted mouth that appeared as if it was trying to scream – but nothing would come out.

Needless to say, I ended up staying up on the third floor and helping Maria clean.

From that day on, I traded in my black patent leather "working woman" heels for a pair of black flats that I found on sale at the local five-store shopping mall, a town over.

Luckily, that day Sophia had come in early – a saving grace. I was sure she must have had a sixth sense telling her something was wrong.

She appeared earlier than the first day I met her with her long flowing hair and adorned in her puffy yet elegant black ski jacket.

"Corrine! Maria!" she excitedly proclaimed. "How are the guests?!"

"Oh, they're fine. We had a toilet issue on the third floor, but Andres fixed it," I replied.

"Good. Oh my! Did I tell you about the deer by our house the other day?" Sophia said in her comforting French accent.

"No, I love deer!" Maria squealed through her endearing Spanish accent.

"Me too!" I beamed.

That seemed to cut the tension.

She and Mr. Crystal lived about ten minutes from the Mansion down a winding private road through the forest.

"Oh yes, we have all kinds of animals, rabbits, a bear, deer. I see the deer every day almost when I have my coffee in the morning. The squirrel shows up soon after the deer, jumping from one bird feeder to another."

Sophia, Maria, and I laughed about all the cute and funny animals she described to us. Most particularly the squirrel that was notorious for stealing all the bird seed.

I wondered how they had such a beautiful home since the Inn made little to no money, and they still managed to have a castle in France.

"We even have a black wolf."

"A black wolf?" Maria asked.

"Yes, a black wolf. I swear, oh my, one day I looked out my window, and she was just standing there, staring at me, her and her two wolf cubs."

"That's enough, Sophia. Let the girls go home!" said Mr. Crystal, as he appeared out of the office from what seemed like nowhere.

He had an odd habit of showing up at just the right time.

CHAPTER 4

After the holiday weekend, Mr. Crystal and I had another "heart to heart." And by "heart to heart," I mean him silently waiting for me at 9 am in the blue wingback chair that sat across from the vintage leather sofa, staring down toward the floor.

"How are you doing? Is everything ok?" he asked as he slowly lifted his head up, his gloomy eyes looking back at me with an empty stare.

I thought maybe he was warming up to me a little.

"Well, everything is fine. But I'm just curious about the. Um. Ghosts." I blurted out. I just couldn't bite my tongue anymore and thought since maybe he was warming up to me a bit, kind of, he could tell me more. Maybe he would have an explanation for the strange things that were beginning to happen.

"The only two ghosts here are you and I," he said as he got up, put on the same tattered baseball cap with embroidered tennis racquets he usually wore along with a worn brown sports jacket, and shuffled away without leaving me anytime to ask more questions.

...

As the weather got colder and the season began to die down (or what little season we had), fewer tourists asked for tours that I wasn't allowed to give, which gave me less and less to do. So, I decided to do some "Fall Spring Cleaning" to try to give the Inn some curb appeal.

One day in late fall, I was cleaning the glass windows adjacent to the two imposing doors at the front entrance of the lobby and noticed a couple wandering about the grounds. I waved, and they waved back. I didn't see any sign of Mr. Crystal, so I thought this was the perfect time to sneak in a break and talk to someone – anyone.

Andres was never to be found and always too busy to talk, anyway.

Maria had never come back to work after the day Sophia surprised us in the afternoon. I wasn't sure if it was the creepy drawing of the ghost-like figure she found in the guest room on the third floor, or Sophia telling us about the black wolves that finally scared her off for good. Or – if it was possibly something more sinister?

Anyway, as I made my way out to the front of the Mansion, the couple smiled and greeted me. "Oh, hi! Do you work here? We're just looking around."

"I do!" I exclaimed, and we started chatting. The woman said I reminded her of her daughter, a writer, and it opened up an entire can of worms. We talked for about fifteen minutes while her husband made his way around the property, taking note of several old monuments that were dated 1854, 1860, 1864, and so on.

"Are you familiar with the history of this place?" the woman asked.

"Not so much, but a friend told me there's a lot of Civil War history," I replied, thinking back to the seemingly enchanted black and white photographs.

"I don't doubt it," her husband said as he walked over from the statues. "We're just up visiting from Florida, staying with friends down the road. But we do know the history of Glowing Rock. Have you heard of Dr. Ribkin?"

"Mmmm, no, I haven't…"

"You should look him up. This town used to be a haven back in the day for sick people. Dr. Ribkin believed that people with yellow fever could come here to get well again. That's how the place became a popular spot. I believe this Inn was also a hospital during the Civil War."

Creepy, I thought. *If it was a popular place for people with yellow fever, how many people had died here trying to get well?*

"Well, that's enough of that. My husband's a bit of a history enthusiast. Good luck with your writing. You should check out our daughter's blog. It's about food," said the woman, as she pulled her jacket tighter, shielding herself from the late fall winds.

When I got home that evening, I googled Dr. Ribkin, and that *is* how Glowing Rock was established; for the sick and dying in the early 1800s.

1808 to be exact.

Eerie.

I had wanted to work at a haunted hotel, but not this kind of haunted.

CHAPTER 5

As the leaves began to change and the cold rolled in, I started to see a muster of crows. There were five, six, sometimes seven of them. When I would leave the Inn at night, they would sit on the dimly lit lamp posts and fly away as I would drive past them down the long winding driveway up to the small two-lane road that ran along the property line.

Thanksgiving was quickly arriving, and the blanket of darkness would come earlier each night, sweeping in an unprecedented cold for the small mountain town.

On my drive into the Mansion every morning in early November, the crows would swoop down and land on top of a lamppost draped in thick fog. Some would land on the dreary-looking vast front lawn that I had convinced Mr. Crystal to have mowed late summer. Their dark black shadows peered at me through the heavy haze. It's almost as if the crows would be waiting for me.

The past couple of months at the Mansion, I had been trying to spend as much time outdoors as possible, since it felt less foreboding outside. I'd sweep off fallen leaves from the two large porches and walkways. But the cold mountain air had arrived, forcing me inside the Inn for warmth.

It seemed notably colder than the past few I had spent in the South.

I had somewhat managed to organize the mess of the front desk area into some clear plastic bins of old notes, one pile of overpriced ski gear magazines, the cash drawer & check-in books – so I enjoyed spending more time there. But as winter grew closer, the lobby and check-in desk became increasingly colder, as did the rest of the Mansion.

The lobby was barely tolerable without a warm winter jacket and constant refill of hot coffee. The only warm room was the breakfast and bar room, where Mr. Crystal began to linger. He'd sit in the oversized armchair that sat closest to the fire, usually staring off into the distance, almost as if he was watching something – or someone.

The large fireplace was now illuminated daily, the flames and embers reflecting off the copper-tiled ceiling.

"Corrine, dear!" He would call from the breakfast room, as I sat at the front desk, warming my hands with my oversized scarf.

"Make us some tea? Will you?"

The tea had to be made from the tea jar in the spice section of the cold, dark, and unused kitchen (except for when Mr. Crystal made his stews or leftover pizza warmed & topped with eggs). The loose tea leaves had to be boiled for hours and were as black as the crows that lined the long, winding driveway.

Mr. Crystal would insist I sit with him and drink the concoction by the roaring fire.

The conversation was routinely bizarre and could span from anything from his hopes and dreams for the Inn to peculiar questions about my family and childhood.

"Order me a hat!" he randomly belted out one afternoon as we were drinking tea.

I moved from the oversized couch in front of the roaring fire into the office where I had had my job interview, Mr. Crystal shuffling in behind me.

"I want a red one – the warmest one you can find!" he said, as I scrolled through the results for "red men's winter hats."

"So there's this one that's nice, it's like $25, or there's this one that's $100."

"Order me the most expensive one you can find!"

"Ok," I replied, trying to hide the hint of irritation in my voice. I didn't really feel like searching for red hats for hours, looking for the most expensive one on the entire internet, especially since it was after 4:30 and I wanted to go home on time.

"Looks like the $100 one it is!" I declared, as he handed me his credit card.

Again, an eerie feeling rushed over me, as if Mr. Crystal had known something I hadn't – as if he was preparing for some unprecedentedly ferocious snowstorm.

"Why would you need such a warm hat in North Carolina? Glowing Rock barely gets half a snowflake," I whispered under my breath as he shuffled back to the worn chair next to the fire.

Eventually, Mr. Crystal insisted we walk to the quaint bakery down the road for a veggie pizza every other day or so. He would shuffle slowly, with a slight limp, and I would walk patiently beside him.

On our way down to the bakery, we would walk the winding driveway lined with a small stone brick wall, then down the weeping willow tree-lined road. The short walk on the road that led to the village took us past the (mostly vacant) apartments that I assumed the summer help stayed (when the hotel actually had a single living soul in it – besides Mr. Crystal & I).

Mr. Crystal owned those too, and had mentioned me living there a few times in passing so that I could "be across the street from the Mansion for emergencies" since Sophia and he didn't like driving through their large private forest that led to their house during the night. He said too many deer would dart out in the middle of the road, making it dangerous for either of them to drive at such late hours.

"You wouldn't have to commute to work!" he exclaimed one afternoon, as we slowly made our way back to the Mansion from the bakery, small pizza boxes in hand.

"Wouldn't that be wonderful..." he mumbled as he pulled his new burgundy wool hat further down over his head.

I enjoyed my cottage on the side of the mountain that I had been renting and didn't want to move. It was the perfect one-bedroom, with hardly any neighbors in earshot, and just far enough away from the Inn to not be "called in for emergencies" in the middle of the night. I liked spending my evenings out on my porch in the summer watching the blue ghost fireflies or curled up on the couch in the winter, with my small fireplace sending flickers into the air as I journaled or wrote short ghost stories in solitude.

Not long after the lengthy and daunting conversations with Mr. Crystal began – I started to feel ill. One night, right before Thanksgiving, I was up all night with the chills & couldn't stop vomiting no matter how hard I tried. Finally, I called my friend Anya from Mable's, early in the morning, and she drove me to the hospital. They gave me a sedative to calm me down, some fluids, and then Anya drove me home.

The next day I was back to work at the Mansion.

I had really begun to enjoy the pay raise. I didn't want to risk getting fired for staying out sick, knowing how irritated Mr. Crystal sounded on the phone the day before when I was in the hospital and called out.

CHAPTER 6

The following week at the Inn was amazing. Mr. Crystal would greet me with a fresh-made breakfast of scrambled eggs with toast and a look of cheer on his face. He would usually leave for the day early in the afternoon, to avoid driving back to their estate in the dark. Sophia hardly came in that week, leaving me alone at the Inn.

I was feeling pleasantly refreshed and didn't feel like I had been sick at all.

Sophia came in more often – right as a bone-chilling cold front did. She would arrive as the darkness blanketed the Mansion, explaining that she wanted to show me some more of the bookkeeping.

Monday, she came in with her signature baked apple strudel, which I devoured while she explained more of the financials of the Inn to me and how to submit tax reports.

She came in around the same time on Tuesday, and we continued our work side by side at the front desk.

It was nearing 6:30, and the wind was particularly gusty. A frigid draft crept through the windows and engulfed the air inside the Mansion; only a solitary space heater kept us semi-warm.

"You already know that reservations go in the front desk journals and reservation book. When the front desk journals get near the end, let me know, and I will bring in a new—"

WHAM!

A thunderous knocking sound rang from the front doors. Usually, only one man used the cumbersome brass door knocker, and he came once a month and always before 5 pm to pay his rent for a home in the village he rented from Mr. Crystal & Sophia. So, the loud knock came as a surprise.

"I wonder who it is?" Sophia said as she looked up at me from the front desk log with a perplexed look.

"I don't know. That's weird. I'll make sure it's locked," I replied and walked out from behind the desk through the dimly lit lobby, past the two blue wingback chairs, and over to the grand front door. I peered out the fish-eyed lens of the peephole in the door, but all I could see was darkness. I unlocked the large gold-plated deadbolt and flung open the massive door, hoping to catch someone by surprise – I was convinced it would be someone of the undead.

The wind howled and bit through the small holes in my navy-blue sweater. The air carried a feeling of unease. So, I shut the oversized front door and relocked it, slowly walking back toward the front desk where Sophia was, leaving time to digest what had just happened.

"Who was it?" she asked, with her soft French accent.

"No one. There was no one there." I barked, a wave of irritation beginning to grow in me. Something about Sophia began to seem guileful, and I wondered if the roaring, unexpected, and unexplained knock was meant to be an ominous warning.

"A ghost, maybe?" she said with a slight laugh.

"Yeah. Maybe the Holy Ghost," I retorted, unamused.

...

On Wednesday evening, as nightfall began to set in, the phone rang, and Mr. Crystal quickly answered it.

I could hear him in the office from where I was sitting in the tall wooden chair behind the front desk.

"Yes. Yes... Ok. Yes." Mr. Crystal said. I heard a beep as he hung up, and then he shuffled out to where I was sitting at the check-in counter.

"I must leave now; something has come up. Would you stay until Sophia comes in?"

"Sure," I replied. I was paid hourly and didn't have a dog, boyfriend, or even a house mouse to get home to, so I figured I would stay and make some extra cash to help pay down my staggering student loans.

Knowing the bar needed a little TLC (plus, the restaurant and bar room stayed warm, unlike the rest of the Inn with the roaring fireplace constantly brewing warm embers), I went through and cleared out the cooler behind the bar, opening each half-empty wine bottle and pouring out the sour contents. I sifted through beer bottles that looked like they were from centuries ago and wiped up old, sticky spills. I organized all of the cocktail napkins into one neat pile.

Next, I headed into the kitchen. Mr. Crystal usually liked me to clean the Inn's first floor in the mornings, right when I got in. He said it "built character like the military did" and would remind me of his time in the Air Force. I felt like reminding him that I didn't sign up for the military, but instead, I would clean with no complaint. Mopping the tile and hardwood floors throughout and hand washing the heavy Le Creuset braisers, greasy frying pans, and overabundance of teacups, saucers, and silverware that would mysteriously pile up throughout the day.

Since I was still waiting for Sophia to arrive, I decided to get a head start on the dishes that I'd have to wash in the morning. I put on my much less expensive version of Sophia's puffy black jacket. I zipped it up tight to keep me warm in the now (always) abnormally frigid kitchen.

I turned the tap on extra hot and put on the dishwashing gloves I brought in from home. My nails were already beginning to look dry and brittle from all the hard work, not to mention that I hadn't had a manicure in months. (Mr. Crystal had a strict 'no nail polish and no lipstick' policy.)

The water heated the exterior of the yellow dish gloves, a welcoming warmth to my chilled bones. The large steel kitchen sink sat below the oversized window looking out over the gloomy and barren parking lot. I stared out, half looking at my reflection and half imagining myself outside in the chilled and shadowy fall atmosphere. The longer I stood there, the more I couldn't shake the feeling that I was being watched. The sense of unease began to grow from the pit of my stomach and spread out into my blood and through my veins.

I slowly turned off the water, removed the dish gloves, hung them over the side of the large stainless-steel sink, and walked delicately back toward the front desk.

I reached into my handbag that hung from the corner of the chair behind the desk and clicked the side of my phone to check the time.

7 pm.

That can't be right... I thought. Why would Sophia be so late?

I fished around in my bag and found a slightly crushed granola bar. "That'll work," I mumbled to myself. I certainly didn't want to go back into the kitchen to find something to eat, since I couldn't shake the feeling of being watched by someone or something.

Not to mention, the fruit that Sophia had been bringing in as of late seemed to turn moldy within days. Anytime I reached for a grape or handful of berries, it would be coated with bits of fuzzy white or half-shriveled into a sphere of black mold.

Only a few minutes after I had sat down at the check-in desk – I received a call from Sophia.

"Corrine, someone has called and said there are lights on on the third floor, can you go and turn them off, please? I will be in soon, I just," and the reception on the phone became fuzzy.

"Of cour—," I began to reply, but was cut off mid-sentence.

Click.

I wonder who would call about the lights on the third floor? I thought but knew how serious Mr. Crystal was about keeping all the lights off - so, I grabbed the large keyring for the third floor and headed up.

As I made my way up to each landing, I switched on the sconces and chandeliers to illuminate the pitch-black Mansion. When I got up to the third floor, before I switched on the lights that lined the walls of the long hallway – I noticed a luster coming from the corner at the end of the hallway.

It appeared as if the door to the room at the end of the hallway was left wide open.

I turned the third-floor hallway lights on and hesitantly walked to the right, toward the seemingly opened door – the old floors creaking with each footstep.

As I neared the illuminated room, I stared at my reflection in the window at the end of the hallway, the antique glass distorting my features and shape.

When I got to #319, I stopped at the open door to the small room and peered in, seeing that the light was coming from the bathroom.

Why is the door open? I wondered. *The doors are always locked shut...*

#319 was one of the smaller rooms, and we never rented it. It was supposed to be used as an 'emergency room' in case we were over-booked (but that never happened, obviously).

#319 had two twin beds that sat side by side, draped in floral bedspreads. A small antique brown nightstand with a solitary lamp and an oval blue rug were nestled in between the beds.

I gulped for a breath of courage and entered – making my way from the bedroom area into the small bathroom on the left. Once I got into the bathroom, I reached for the metal string hanging from the lights above the medicine cabinet when it hit me – a foul smell. Something that smelled old and rotted and reminded me of death, even though I had no idea what death *actually* smelled like.

The thought that the Inn used to be a hospital flashed before my eyes, and the twin beds that loomed in the reflection of the mirror on the medicine cabinet reminded me of what John from Mable's had said about his friends hearing voices of children on the third floor.

I quickly pulled the tiny metal string to turn the light off in the small bathroom and turned around to rush out of the room. Once I got to the hallway, I realized that all of the lights had shut off in the hallways and staircases.

"This can't be happening..." I stammered, assuming the power had gone out... hoping the power had gone out.

As much as I wanted to run back downstairs, the hallway was now only illuminated by a sliver of the moon that crept in through the oversized restoration glass windows at the end of the hallway and near the grand staircase that led back to the first floor.

Once I got to the landing, I grabbed onto the railing and peered over it to look down to the first floor, to see that the lights we're still on – seemingly only on the main level of the Inn.

The power was not out – but somehow all of the lights on the staircase, second, and third floor, had been turned off.

Frightened beyond words and with a feeling of deceit and mystery lingering in the air from what had just happened & the ominous knocking at the front doors the night before, I remembered how Sophia had mentioned that every time a front desk notebook was full, they used a new one. I thought staying behind the check-in desk and burying my head in a notebook might offer me some refuge.

Where the heck is Sophia? I thought to myself, as I kneeled down behind the desk and slid open the wooden cabinet. Next to the files of files and old ski magazines was a small pile of black and white composition books that I had organized but never taken the time to look through. Yet now, something was gravitating me toward them.

I grabbed the stack of three notebooks and sat back onto the wooden front desk chair, zipping up my jacket even tighter. I started with the oldest book, which dated back a few years, and began to read the notes page by page. There were mainly random notes about financials, who had paid what when, and random reservation dates. But, the further I got into the book, the more I began to see my name: "Corrine; 10/22." The closer I got to the current date, the more I saw my name scribbled in the book with a random date next to it, from years prior.

"Corrine 12/5."

"Corrine 3/13."

There must have been at least a dozen entries with my name and a date next to it.

Sometimes it would be in cursive; other times, it would look like someone else's handwriting, sometimes by yet another person.

Page by page, I read every note in every front desk book until I got to the end of the last one; and there it was – my name with my birthdate. "Corrine; 7/10."

July 10th was only a little over a month before I had my first interview at the Mansion.

"What the freaking hell?" I fumed, as I slammed the notebook shut. I grabbed the new notebook to make sure I hadn't completely lost my mind.

The day I started, they had begun documenting in a new journal.

So many things began to race through my mind... *Maybe someone else used to stay at the Inn a lot, and their name was Corrine? Maybe they have a distant relative named Corrine – they like to remember the dates she called?* So many scenarios were swirling in my head.

Not more than two minutes later, the phone rang.

"Crystal Inn," I answered, trying not to sound perturbed.

"Corrine!" Mr. Crystal exclaimed. "Why are you still there?"

"Well, I thought I was supposed to wait until Sophia came in?"

"No! No... Go home, dear. Sophia isn't coming in tonight."

Click.

As soon as he hung up the phone, I grabbed my handbag and coffee mug and hurriedly walked out to my car. As I approached my small white crossover, the light in the lamppost directly above me began to flicker. It went completely out, leaving a pocket of darkness where I was standing in the frigid night air.

CHAPTER 7

The following days I felt unexplainably stranger and stranger. I got into a routine of dusting off old paintings up the dimly illuminated grand red staircase or vacuuming the ornate Persian rugs & hallways – anything to keep my mind off how unstable I felt.

It was as if my night alone at the Inn had unleashed some type of fear or spell – or perhaps a combination of both.

One day at the landing of the steps that led down to the lobby, where an outlet lay hidden behind a small table lined with antique books about war, it hit me. When I kneeled down to plug in the vacuum, I felt like not just the room was spinning but the entire universe. I could barely walk and had to almost crawl back down the steps to the front desk. The feeling lingered for days. I would walk around the wide hallways and corridors, stumbling between them, unable to grasp a footing.

"You shouldn't be driving like that." Andres, the groundskeeper said, one day when he came up to the front desk to ask for a spare key to one of the apartments across the street.

"It's not safe. You could get in an accident. Stay home for a while, and don't drive." he emphasized with a worried look.

I leaned up against the edge of the check-in counter. I held one hand on the cherry wood top for stability, meagerly attempting to mask my weakness.

That evening I saw Sophia as I was leaving for the night. We met halfway along the dark, winding driveway – where the crows usually would land. I slowed down as I saw her large black Cadillac come around the bend. (She and Mr. Crystal drove the same style, same color car.)

"Corrine!" she exclaimed.

"Hi, Sophia," I said weakly, noticing what I sensed to be a false look of concern on her face.

"I'm not feeling that well, actually. I keep falling, and it's really weird. I don't know."

"On no! That doesn't sound good."

"Yeah, would you mind if I went to the doctor's office tomorrow morning? The hospital said I should follow up with my doctor...."

"No, no... you go. Stay healthy!" Sophia said in a tone that didn't seem very genuine. "We're slow anyway, now that the winter is coming.". "Bye!" she said, and drove off toward the Inn.

...

The following day I went to see my physician. The nurse always asked me what kind of pie we had that week at Mable's while she was checking my vitals. She and her husband were big fans of the oversized apple caramel drizzle that we always had an overabundance of in the fall & winter.

"How's work?" she asked.

"I actually got a new job! I'm working at an inn over in Glowing Rock."

"Really?" she asked, as the tone in her voice changed, and she slowly and gently wrapped the blood pressure cuff around my arm.

"So, is it the one over by Ravenswood Road? It's got that white wrap-around porch and has about seven or eight rooms?" she inquired nonchalantly but with a seemingly worried tone, without making eye contact.

"No, it's the really old building up on the hill. The Crystal Inn. It used to be the Glowing Rock Inn a while back."

"Oh. Well, we'll need to run some blood work since you keep falling; make sure everything's all right," the nurse said, reaching into a box full of small vials.

She began to tell me about how she and her family used to go to the Glowing Rock Inn when she was younger on Easter for brunch, the kids used to play and scavenge for eggs on the vast front lawn.

I imagined what were now old, dilapidated pavilions – were filled to the brim with families dressed in colorful ensembles, laughing and celebrating. The picnic tables sprawled with bright baskets overflowing with equally as bright eggs and oversized chocolate bunnies.

"Some of the locals around here, you know the older locals, like my parents and some other people, think it's haunted."

"Yeah, I've heard," I nervously laughed and thought back to John from the pie shack and his story about the voices on the third floor, not to mention my most recent unexplainable experiences.

"Well, not just haunted but possessed or something. A lot of them won't even go there anymore, let alone talk about it. I just thought you should know," she said.

...

My bloodwork came back fine, and my illness and uncontrollable falling became a medical mystery.

"Avoid caffeine," my doctor ordered.

That wasn't happening. Drinking coffee was my only saving grace from having to partake with Mr. Crystal and his tea-drinking psychoanalysis sessions.

"Join me for some tea," he would declare every day around 2 pm.

"Oh, no thanks, I have my coffee already made. Thank you," I would answer and remind him that it was always nice to have coffee out for any potential guests that showed up at the Inn.

That didn't stop him from insisting I sit and talk with him, however.

The longer his strange questions continued as I sat on the couch facing the fireplace, the worse I felt physically, and the more coffee I needed to make it through afternoons, especially right before my drive home.

I thought I was fine to drive, but I wasn't. One night after work, I decided to swing by a coffee shop for a latte and late-night holiday treat. *Maybe something with lots of sugar*, I thought.

The further away from the Mansion I drove, the weaker and more disoriented I became. I felt again like the world around me was spinning and that I was losing track of time and space.

Once I got into the next town over, the weather quickly became precariously cold, snowy, and icy – mid-drive. I was so delirious that I had come to a red light but didn't even notice the color. I had gone too fast around the corner, trying to avoid the oncoming traffic. My compact crossover careened on the ice and fishtailed into a metal divider on the corner of a small strip mall that housed a vacuum store and barbershop.

The next day my friend Anya drove me into work. She was a new mom and had taken some time off except for a few shifts on the weekends, so luckily she had the freedom to keep driving me everywhere.

"Do you think everything is ok at the hotel?" she asked.

"What do you mean?" I replied softly as I stared blankly off into the thick woods and all too familiar cemeteries on our drive in.

"Well, I don't know. I mean, maybe there could be something going on there. Like, maybe some kind of dark magic or witchcraft? Do you think maybe you should stop working there? I've seen that guy's wife around town at the produce market. She always has this far-off look in her eyes. I don't know – the place is creepy."

"No, I think I'll be alright. I think she just misses her family in France," I whispered, mustering the energy to make the walk from Anya's car to the Mansion's back door, coffee in hand.

"Ok, well, be safe. Let me know how you're doing or if you need a ride or whatever."

"Thank you, Anya," I said, giving her a half-worried smile and pulling the hood to my oversized black parka over my damp hair.

I walked to the front desk and put my bag and coffee down, wrapping my ivory-colored knit scarf tighter around my neck. I hoped Mr. Crystal wouldn't appear anytime soon.

I should have known better from the over-powering breakfast-like smell wafting from the kitchen.

Not moments later, Mr. Crystal came shuffling to the front lobby down the blood-red corridor with a plate, fork, and knife in hand.

"Eat! Eat! You must eat to stay healthy and strong!" Mr. Crystal belted as he dropped the plate with two over-done tuna patties in front of me next to the phone and call log composition book.

Interesting choice, I thought, as I disregarded his comments and took a gulp of courage while I picked up the fork and knife, knowing he would be offended if I didn't eat the crispy-looking cakes.

"Corrine!" he shouted from his oversized chair in front of the fire, not moments after

I had finished forcing down the fishcakes. "Come sit with me!"

I grabbed my cup of coffee, thinking it might mask the lingering taste of grease and fish, which was making me feel even more uneasy, and headed into the breakfast room.

Oddly enough, the lights were all on, and the few that had usually illuminated the large room were lit even brighter.

"Now we have number nine. Naturally, you would want to live on the end. It's such a nice unit. You'd be far away from all the other tenants," Mr. Crystal explained in a matter-of-fact kind of way.

By other tenants, he meant three. Three apartments were rented in two buildings that held sixteen available units for rent.

"You can stay there now since you can't drive; you can just walk to work. It doesn't matter the weather. How wonderful of a thing you can be so close!"

Since I had no car and could barely drive anyway due to my ever-intensifying and unexplainable vertigo, I agreed.

"Andres will take you to your cabin and help you move your stuff today. Take the day and do that – I will pay you both your normal wages. Plus, here's $100 to get some new things you might need for the move," Mr. Crystal said as he handed me a crisp $100 bill that he had pulled from a plastic bag full of other $100 bills mixed with an overabundance of loose change and other bills of various amounts.

Soon after, as Andres was driving me over to my cabin through the winding back roads of the mountains, he glanced over at me from the corner of his eye.

"Miss Corrine, I like you. You're a nice person." He paused for a moment, looking straight ahead.

"Sophia – I don't like her. You can't trust them. You just go. You do your job, but don't trust them. Especially Sophia."

"Ok," I acknowledged, thinking I knew what he meant. Or at least - to what degree.

...

My first night in #9 was cold. Freezing cold. I could barely sleep. The heater was definitely not working.

The next day Mr. Crystal sent Andres over to fix the heat and lights, after I mentioned how cold and dark it was. Half of the bulbs were either burnt out, or the socket itself was broken.

"Hey Andres, you remember what you were saying yesterday about Sophia?" I asked while he was mid-fix on a light bulb socket.

He stopped, turned towards me, and stared intently into my eyes. He didn't say a word, but somehow, I knew he didn't want to talk about it right then, almost as if someone was listening.

...

The second night at #9 was much warmer. I decided to get some unpacking done and settle in. I kept the front porch light on as I put some knick-knacks out on the little shelf in the kitchen and on top of the dresser in the bedroom, then lit a candle to make the apartment feel homier.

Not long after dinner time came a knock on my door. Under the porch light stood a petite blonde woman, wearing a hefty-looking winter coat, her hair pulled way up in a high ponytail. I assumed it was one of the three neighbors that lived in the ghost-like village. She, however, was nothing ghost-like.

"Do you need anything, doll?" she asked.

"I'm Cherri; we spoke on the phone a while back. I used to work for Old Man Crystal. I still rent from him now. He thinks I stole his spices."

"Oh no, I'm ok. I'm just unpacking, and..." I trailed off as I looked around, realizing I had no real food.

"How about I just pick you up a few things?" Cherri asked with her kind demeanor.

I humbly agreed, and we made small talk as I invited her in for a cup of coffee while I rummaged around for a loose twenty in the bottom of my handbag.

Not long after, Cherri returned with two plastic grocery bags in hand and handed me a small piece of torn paper with her phone number written down on it.

"We're all just a few apartments down. I'm up in #13, Bill is in #17, and Walter in #12. The numbers don't really make sense. You should be #1, not #9, since you're the first one down here on the end, but don't let that confuse you. Just call me if you need anything." She smiled and walked off into the dark, back to the other side of the small apartment complex that was divided in the middle by a small run-down laundry room.

The next morning, I got up early to leave some extra time for my walk over to the Mansion, across the road, and up the winding driveway. I had all my hair and makeup done, outfit on, and was just about to pull a piping hot mug of cinnamon-flavored oatmeal out of the microwave that Cherri had bought for me - when my phone rang.

It was Sophia.

"How are you feeling?" she asked.

"Well, I'm ok; I just feel weak. I don't know. I think I'm doing better I was just about to eat and head out to—"

Before I could finish my thought, she interrupted. "You know, I often feel run down. I never wanted to run an inn."

"Sophia, I just have to ru—"

There was no interrupting her. 9:00 turned into 9:15, and I was late for work, feeling exponentially more drained the longer she talked.

For the next few days, my phone would ring around the same time every day, right before I was about to eat or leave.

Her timing was impeccable, to say the least.

Every day I was late for work, and Mr. Crystal would shuffle past me without saying a word, clearly irritated - as I was rushing in.

CHAPTER 8

We were expecting a heavy snowstorm one night mid-week, so Sophia insisted she drive me home to #9 from the Mansion after work. She had arrived much earlier than usual, proclaiming that the storm was on its way and that she had stocked up on groceries.

"You'll have to sit in the back; my groceries are in the front," she stated as we walked out into the chilly fall air that felt more like winter.

"Ummm, ok," I mumbled as I opened the heavy door to her Cadillac and crawled into the back.

The quick drive to the apartments across from the Mansion was nothing short of bizarre as Sophia shot me expressionless glances from the rear-view mirror. I tried not to look back and make eye contact, so stared straight ahead and watched the winding driveway & vast lawn roll by – the crows nowhere in sight that dark afternoon.

"Here you go," she said, pulling up in front of #9, putting her car in park, turning around, and handing me a bag from the market.

"In case it snows so much you can't make it out, here are some fruits and stuff," she said, with a slightly twisted yet still pretty smile. I definitely was beginning to feel some kind of extra weird vibes from her. Still, I wasn't going to pass up a bag full of fresh berries and bananas (presuming they hadn't rotted yet).

I thanked her, got out, and pushed closed the heavy door to her black Cadillac, behind me. It was right before sundown, and the sky was filled with swirling black clouds in a sea of dark grey. I had never seen the sky like that before.

Not a minute after I walked in the door to the apartment, my phone rang.

"Hey! It's Cherri. So there's a big storm coming through. We're all ordering pizza down here at Walters' – just come on down if the power goes out. Or if you're bored. Either way. No pressure, love."

It was nice to hear a kind and somewhat familiar voice. I thanked Cherri and said I would let them know if I needed anything.

"Oh, and I just want to let you know – don't let Sophia keep you on the phone all morning. She'll suck the life right out of you, and you'll always be late to work. And remember, just walk on down if ya need anything," she insisted.

The winter storm came in strong that evening, and the snow continued to fall all night and into the day.

The phone rang that morning like clockwork. I didn't feel like answering it and was abnormally tired. All I wanted to do was sit on my small love seat and watch the large snowflakes fall outside the oversized picture windows with my hands wrapped around a warm cup of coffee. I looked down at the piece of scrap paper with Cherri's number on it and, choosing not to heed her advice, reluctantly answered the phone. It was Sophia.

That morning, our conversation must have gone on for hours. And by conversation, I mean Sophia complaining about Mr. Crystal and the Mansion and me going "mmm hmmm," attempting to mask my mumbled yawns. By the time she stopped talking, I barely had enough energy to put my shoes on.

I'll just call it a sick day, I thought.

I tried calling the Mansion, but the phone went to the answering machine, so I hung up and figured I'd call back later.

My perfectly hot coffee was now cold, so I decided to put some comfy clothes on and crawled back into bed.

...

"Corrine...." I heard, in a soft voice, close to my ear. "Corrine..."

I woke up to a dark room. I thought I must have been dreaming but soon realized I had slept the entire day away.

I got out of bed, put on some slippers, and slowly shuffled into the kitchen to look at the time on the stove – it was 6:00 pm, although it didn't feel like it.

As I stood by the refrigerator contemplating what to eat, cold air swept through under the door that led out to the side porch, and the outside light began to flicker through the sea of heavy snowflakes.

It was odd.

More than odd.

I hadn't remembered leaving the side porch light on, but it was a new apartment, so I chalked it up as maybe just flipping the wrong switch. But yet, an eerie and unsettling feeling lingered – I felt like I was being watched, again.

This seemed like an awfully strong storm for the South, I thought. Then, I had a flashback to dusting off some of the antique Civil War pictures from the hallway near the lobby of the Mansion. One of the black and white photos had soldiers lined up on the front lawn when they were stationed there, holding their rifles in snow that was almost up to their knees.

The thought of the image combined with the overbearing draft made me shiver. I went back into the bedroom to layer on a sweatshirt, thinking back to what my mom always used to say when we would have particularly cold nights in Maine – "Put a sweater on and drink some hot chocolate."

I didn't have any hot chocolate, but I did have coffee.

My coffee pot had broken in the move to #9. To make do, I had been wrapping some coffee grounds in a filter with a twist tie I had found at the bottom of one of my yet-to-be-emptied moving boxes. Bringing some water to a boil in a pot, I dropped the coffee grounds in and waited for the water to slowly turn into a dark brown.

Standing in front of the stove, I felt another rush through the cold air and then a loud bang on the side door that let out from the kitchen.

"Are you scared, Corrine?" An audible voice that sounded eerily like Sophia echoed into the brisk winter air that had crept through the cracks and made its way into the apartment. The voice sounded as if it was emanating from the walls and ceiling.

I ran over to the brown moving box by the door from where I had retrieved the twist tie and hurriedly grabbed a large chef's knife, gripping it so tight in my right hand that my palm began to turn blue.

Knife in hand, I moved back from the door over to the small shelf on the other side of the kitchen where I had left my phone to charge. Still gripping the knife with my right hand, I picked up my cell phone in my left, thinking I would call someone, anyone, maybe Anya, maybe my mother, possibly even the sheriff's department.

There was no service.

Every morning prior, there had been enough service for Sophia to call and keep me on the phone for hours. But now, mid-snowstorm and horrifying haunting voice, there wasn't even one bar. Since I hadn't had the time (or energy, for that matter) to set up the WiFi, I couldn't use the internet to get In touch with anyone, either.

When I put the fully charged (but useless) phone back on the shelf, I noticed the small piece of paper with Cherri's phone number on it. I quickly layered on my black, puffy, Sophia-style jacket & a pair of boots – turned off the burner to the stove, put the shiny silver knife in the inside pocket of my coat, and headed out into the frosty night air to try to find some refuge at Cherri's.

I walked out the front door and to my left since all the other apartments were in that direction. I remembered what Cherri had said about the numbers and how they could get confusing. My mind felt foggy, but I kept focused on the number thirteen; that's all I needed to find – #13.

The harder I looked, the more confusing my search became. #12 turned into #8, which led me up a set of stairs, twice. *Hadn't I just been to this one?* I thought, feeling more and more uneasy and disoriented.

Finally, I found a staircase lined with multi-colored crystals. The porch light at the top of the stairs illuminated the gleaming gold house numbers that said #13.

I put one foot onto the first step and felt a rush of cold wind blow through the air, carrying off any ounce of energy I had left with it. I melted to the ground but was able to break my slow fall by planting my palms onto the icy and snowy cement of the walkway.

I felt a pullback toward #9, the apartment Mr. Crystal had assigned me. It felt like it was a magnet, and I was the opposite pole, being pulled in by a force beyond my control.

Quickly I got up. As I made my way back to #9, my mind became less hazy.

Feeling defeated, angry, and petrified, I stormed in the front door, through the small living room, down the tiny hallway and into the bathroom, slamming the door behind me, tears starting to stream down my cheeks.

I locked the vintage silver lock on the bathroom door, slid down the adjacent wall, and gripped the sharp knife tight to my chest.

CHAPTER 9

I woke up abruptly the next day with the cold from the tile floor biting through my thin black yoga pants. As I lay there in the fetal position gazing at the bottom of the sink base cabinet, I wondered if I should even get up. I wondered if today would be a repeat of the days prior.

I slowly lifted my head from the floor, pulled the hoodie from my parka down, and hesitantly peered toward the window above the tub to see that it was a sunny and bright day and that the snow had stopped.

I quietly made my way off the floor, then quickly and strategically ran out of the bathroom, back down the small hallway, and into the closet to grab my handbag, making sure my I.D. & credit card were in there.

I hurriedly walked out into the sunny fresh air, not even taking the time to shut the front door to the apartment behind me. The snow was beginning to melt, and my boots sunk into the mixture of mud and slush in the driveway to the apartments that led back to the weeping willow-lined road that led into the village.

Feeling exhaustion engulf me again the further from #9 I got, I thought it might be a good idea to sit outside the bakery and have some coffee to try to wake up and see if I could make any sense of what had transpired the past couple days and months.

When I approached the counter at the bakery to put my coffee order in, the friendly barista that always took Mr. Crystal's and my pizza orders looked at me as though she had seen a ghost.

"Are you ok?" she asked, as I struggled to keep my footing.

"I'm fine, thank you," I said – not feeling fine at all.

"Ok..." she replied, while gazing back at me with a concerned and doubtful look.

I grabbed my coffee and ducked into the restroom at the bakery to splash some cold water on my face. I picked up a small brown paper napkin and looked into the mirror to dry my face off – the reflection staring back at me was unnaturally pale. My black mascara had smudged all around my eyes and clumped into the corners. My hair was disheveled, so I pulled out my hair tie and combed my fingers through it, noticing a few tiny grey hairs that hadn't been there before.

I heard a knock on the door and then the faint voice of the barista. "Hey, are you alright?"

"I'm fine. Just fine," I replied, somewhat apologetically, as I opened the door and made my way back outside of the bakery onto their patio.

Yet again, I felt a pull in the direction of the apartments. Coffee in hand, I dragged my feet, unwilling to succumb to the magnetic draw.

I stopped halfway out of the village, fighting the urge to go back in the direction of apartment #9. Growing increasingly too weak to stand on my own. I sat down on a park bench on the outskirts of Glowing Rock, cold and confused. I stared straight ahead and watched the weeping trees until the sky danced between the sunny day and twilight.

As I glanced down at my hands and saw that they had begun to turn a bluish-purple, a black and white patrol car from the sheriff's department pulled over on the side of the narrow road.

A deputy wearing a dark, navy-blue uniform stepped out of the car and mumbled something into the radio attached to his black bulletproof vest.

He slowly crossed the road and stood in front of me.

"Ma'am? Everything all right?" he asked. "People been sayin you been sittin here all day."

I stared straight ahead in a foggy paralysis.

"It's getting kinda cold for that, ain't it?" he said, as he let out a slight sigh.

"Lady down at the bakery said you work for Mr. Crystal. Want me to give 'em a call?"

"No, no, don't call them," I half-whispered, half pleaded, as a solitary tear began to form and mix with the mascara clumped in the corner of my eye.

"Well, ya can't just sit out here all night, can ya?" he replied as he rocked back and forth on his black leather boots.

As he grabbed his radio and mumbled something quietly while turning his head out of my line of sight, Cherri pulled up in her small silver hatchback.

"Corrine!" she yelled out the window as she pulled up behind the patrol car.

She hopped out and quickly made her way across the street.

"You know her?" the officer asked Cherri.

"We're neighbors. I used to work for Old Man Crystal, too," she replied.

"Can you just step over here to the side for a minute, ma'am?" he asked as he and Cherri moved away, just enough to be out of earshot. The more they spoke, the more the growing looks of concern washed over their faces.

A few minutes later, the burly officer returned to where I was sitting on the bench and stood to my left side.

"Ma'am, we're gonna get you some help, ok? Can you just stand up for me?"

Barely mustering the strength, I stood up from the bench and began to sob.

The officer handcuffed me, lightly wrapped his hand around my upper arm, and guided me to the side of the road where his patrol car was parked.

At that exact moment, Mr. Crystal and Sophia's black Cadillacs passed by each other on the road. Mr. Crystal was driving in the direction of their home in the forest, and Sophia was headed in the direction of the Mansion.

Although I only got a glimpse of her, Sophia appeared to be more youthful and vibrant than before.

I looked toward Cherri, still in a dazed state of confusion and then at my reflection in the patrol car back window. I barely recognized myself as tears streamed down my cheeks and long lines of black mascara formed on my face.

"It's alright, sweetie," she mouthed.

CHAPTER 10

My stay at the hospital lasted a few weeks. Cherri called me the first day I was there, and then dropped off a journal and some colored pens the next day.

A few days later, my mom showed up during visiting hours and suggested I come back with her to Tennessee to 'recover'.

Mom went through all my stuff at #9 and packed it up. John from Mable's and one of his friends helped her load it into a trailer to take back to Tennessee.

I didn't want to go back to the apartment – the thought of it made me shiver.

A few days before I was released from the hospital, my mom brought me some clothes to wear home and some new sparkly eye makeup and shiny pink lip-gloss. I think she felt bad.

By the time I left the hospital, I was heavily medicated. My eyes were tired-looking and heavy with large dark circles that had formed under them, and I had quickly gained at least fifteen pounds as a side effect of the anti-psychotics.

Clumps of my hair had begun to fall out when I would shampoo it in the shower, and thick grey hairs had sprouted in place. It was as if my hair had turned grey overnight. One of the nurses in the hospital helped me cut it – they weren't supposed to, but I think she felt bad, too.

...

The day I left the psychiatric ward to head to Tennessee, it was particularly bright, sunny, and warm. It felt like spring, although it was only the end of January.

I hesitantly put on a t-shirt and defeatedly looked down at my arms – even the skin on my arms looked tired and bloated.

The plan was to meet my mom in Tennessee, but I had to stop by the Mansion on the way out of town, since Mr. Crystal insisted I come in person to pick up my last paycheck.

As I drove up the long winding driveway, I noticed that the crows weren't out at their usual post. In fact, I didn't see any sign of life whatsoever.

I parked in the back of the Inn, like I usually did, and walked under the pergola laced with ivy where I often spent lonely afternoons, sweeping the red quarry tile walkway.

It always felt dark and grim, even outdoors at the Mansion - with no sign of life except an overabundance of cobwebs, weeds, and over-grown grass. This particular day wasn't an exception until I looked down, still in a medi-cation fog, and noticed patches of white lilies that had bloomed all around the otherwise decaying flower beds that lined the entryway.

"I thought flowers only bloomed in spring?" I mumbled as I hesitantly made my way into the Mansion, down the crimson red hallway, past the check-in desk, and into the breakfast room.

Mr. Crystal was sitting in his usual chair, gaz-ing off into the distance.

"Hi, Mr. Crystal," I said, making my way toward the couch in front of the fireplace.

"Corrine!" he exclaimed. "Come sit with me!"

The fireplace wasn't burning that day, and all the lights were off – as they were when I started at the Inn.

Mr. Crystal had a defeated and tired look on his face, and his eyes looked cloudy.

"You don't look like yourself," he stated in a long and drawn-out sort of way. "I mean, you don't look bad— you just don't look like yourself."

"I know," I replied. "They've got me on a lot of medication; it's got some pretty bad side effects."

"You don't need that. Don't let them make you believe you do."

"I'm actually just here to pick up my last paycheck. I'm going to stay at my mom's for a while."

"I think that's a good idea," he said, looking down at the ground and then pulling out his plastic bag of money.

He slowly counted out the bills, grabbed a T.V. remote off the side of his oversized chair, and turned on the news. It was odd - he rarely turned on the T.V. that hung on the other side of the room over the bar.

"Do you have any tea to bring with you to Tennessee?"

"I don't," I replied.

"Go into the kitchen and grab a tin of tea, the dark black kind. It's my gift to you."

"Ok," I said hesitantly as I made my way back through the cold corridors, into the kitchen, and then back into the breakfast room where Mr. Crystal was sitting.

"Do you have ten dollars for that?" he asked.

"I'm sorry?" I replied.

"For the tea. Actually, it's more like $15 at the market."

"Ok..." I said as I fished out $15 from the money he had paid me and handed it to him in exchange for the tea.

"I'll see you on the other side," Mr. Crystal said as a slight friendly smile came across his face. "Now go! Get! Get on with your life!" he shouted and brushed his hand as if to shoo me away.

...

I got up from the couch feeling conflicted, but happy and ready to start on a new part of my life, a new adventure.

"You asked for a haunting, Corrine... you certainly got a haunting," I whispered to myself as I made my way back out to the parking lot.

When I got outside and down the walkway past the out-of-place lilies, I saw Sophia parked next to my car.

She never parked next to my car.

The closer I got, the more I could make out the look on her face – sheer hatred, and anger that seemed to boil over the closer to her I got.

Once I was within ten feet or so, she opened the door of her car, but didn't get out.

"What are you doing here?! We don't want you here! You're a liar and a thief! Everyone in town thinks so too— they told me that." She continued to shout. As mad as she appeared to be, I sensed a slight tone of fear in her voice when it cracked as she was yelling. The strangest thing of all was that her hair seemed to have grown at least three inches in the past few weeks and had a bright sheen to it, as did her skin. She looked pale, yet glowing.

I didn't say a thing but instead shot her a look of disgust and disdain, got into my crossover, rolled the windows down, and turned on some music for my drive.

"Ugh. What a B." I said as I rolled my eyes and drove away, breathing in the fresh mountain air.

CHAPTER 11

The rest of that winter, I spent at my mom's house, healing, spending lots of time hiking in the Tennessee mountains, reading, resting, and working at a breakfast restaurant.

I quickly dumped the many bottles of medication down the toilet and didn't think twice about it.

When the summer came, and I finally felt comfortable in a swimsuit again, I would spend my afternoons at the lake, swimming in the healing waters and watching all the birds that seemed to flock around me. It seemed as though I had built a special bond with the winged creatures ever since the crows at the Mansion would flock to me along the long winding driveway. I would think back and often wonder if they had been messengers – there to warn me of the impending danger.

Toward the end of my summer spent in Lincolnton (a small town outside of Knoxville), I felt healthy and happy. My hair had grown back, the dark circles under my eyes disappeared, and the skin on my body wasn't bloated anymore.

I had saved up enough money to move back to North Carolina and was elated to find a cute little apartment to rent in Glowing Rock, not too far from the village.

That afternoon, after work at the diner, I came home and locked myself in the bathroom. After the haunting at the Mansion, I often still found myself disconnected from the present world and would stare blankly as if I was looking for something I could never seem to find.

As I stared into the mirror, my phone rang and snapped me back into present time, in the canary yellow bathroom at my mom's house. I looked down to see it was Anya from Mable's calling. Excitedly I answered, and we talked about my life in Tennessee and her family and baby.

"Hey, so the strangest thing happened to me the other day," she said. "When I was at Mable's, we were about to close, and I was clearing a table. You know that man that always comes in and asks for extra syrup heated up for precisely thirty seconds but never actually uses any of it?"

"Of course," I laughed.

"Yeah, well, so you know how he usually leaves behind his newspaper spread out all over the table?"

"Yup," I said and laughed again.

"So when I was clearing the table, I noticed that the newspaper was folded neatly and left open to one page... The headline was something like 'Owners Death Leaves Questions' and then went on to talk about Mr. Crystal and his fortune and who will get it, stuff like that."

"Oh wow. Mr. Crystal died?"

"Yeah. But the weird thing is that he had a heart attack..."

"I mean, that's not so weird, Anya - he was like over ninety," I replied.

"Ok, right? But he had a heart attack right in front of that apartment that you were staying in by the Mansion."

"That is weird—" Mid-sentence, the reception to my phone broke up, and a high-pitched array of sounds screeched from it. They were so loud I had to pull it away from me even though Anya was on speakerphone.

"Anya?" I asked, after the screeching noises stopped – slightly jolted. "Did you hear that?"

"Ummm yeah. Also weird," Anya replied, and we laughed it off.

"Well, I'll see you soon when I'm back in town," I said, thinking back to the last day I had seen Mr. Crystal and Sophia.

"Give me a call when you're back. I can't wait," Anya replied and hung up.

Click.

CHAPTER 12

My first night back in North Carolina felt surreal. On the way into the village, I drove past the Inn. Slowing down as I got closer, I tried to get a glimpse of the Mansion through the trees that had begun to lose their leaves. I couldn't see much of the Inn itself but did notice a dim golden light that hadn't been there before, illuminating the large green sign on the road, with white letters that spelled out "Crystal Inn" with a small handwritten "for sale" sign next to it.

Once I got to my new apartment, a few roads down on the other side of the village, as I unpacked and began to get settled in, I wondered if my new apartment would be haunted... Every creak and bump made me jump – and then laugh.

Nothing could compare to what I had been through in the last year.

...

I woke up the next morning feeling peaceful being back in Glowing Rock, but realized I must have forgot to pack any coffee. I rummaged through my moving boxes for an ounce of coffee or anything with caffeine. All I found was the small tin of tea that Mr. Crystal had sold me for $15.00.

"That'll work," I said to myself and half-smiled.

As I sat out on the balcony at my new apartment, overlooking the lake – a solitary crow landed on the railing where I had propped my feet up and stared back at me, blinking periodically, as crows do. It stayed there until I finished my cup of tea and then flew off, cawing loudly.

...

After putting some clothes away and putting out a few knick-knacks, I took a trip to town to do some grocery shopping. The road to the store I usually went to was blocked off because part of it had washed away in the recent heavy rains, so I stopped at the market that

Sophia had been known to shop at since it was right off the detour.

"I hope their fruit isn't all rotting away," I mumbled under my breath and again thought back to my time at the Inn as I pulled into the parking lot.

I started in the fruit section of the store, and to my disbelief, all of the fruit was beyond fresh.

After filling my basket with some blueberries, apples, oat milk, and cereal, I noticed the tins of tea Mr. Crystal always drank. I picked one up to admire it, noticing the price tag of only $8.00. I laughed again thinking back to Mr. Crystal charging me $15.00, and then headed over to the bakery section to pick up some much-deserved post-hiking desserts and bread.

As I picked up a loaf of fresh-baked bread, I looked up to see Sophia standing in front of the pastry case with her signature long wavy dark brown hair and black ski jacket.

"Sophia?" I belted.

As she turned around, she looked as though she was shocked and bewildered, holding a piece of apple strudel wrapped in bakery parchment paper.

"Corrine..." she stammered, looking me up and down. "You look... great. What have you been doing?"

"Your hair..." she continued as she kept looking at me with attempted masked looks of annoyance and disbelief.

After talking on and on about how great I was doing, the look on Sophia's face quickly turned into an expression of worry, and she excused herself.

When I went down the next aisle, I saw her at the checkout, nervously fumbling through her handbag to pay.

...

That night, I decided to take a walk down to the village for some fresh air and to pick up a pizza to go from the bakery for old time's sake. I put my order in for one vegan veggie pizza and decided to take a stroll past the Mansion while it was being prepared.

I stopped at the green and white sign that said "Crystal Inn" and decided not to go further. The sign for the Inn had been half covered in a brown tarp, and a "No Trespassing!" sign had replaced the "for sale" sign.

That's strange timing, I thought, and then walked back down toward the bakery to pick up my pizza.

...

That night I decided to do some online digging about the Inn while simultaneously devouring my pizza & birdwatching on my porch.

Besides the article about Mr. Crystal dying in front of #9, there was another one about the grand opening of the Mansion from nine years ago. A younger-looking Mr. Crystal sat on the sofa by the roaring fireplace in the breakfast room. Sophia, looking about the same age, loomed over him.

The article mentioned the town in France where Sophia had come from, so I decided to do some digging into that.

Initially, I found nothing but continued to look through old articles about inns in that town and stumbled across an article with a picture of Sophia in it, about forty years prior, looking exactly as she did the day I met her. She was standing outside in front of the sign for the inn "Auberge de l'Etoile", which was surrounded by white lilies.

The more I dug, the more I found – at that very same inn in France, a lady who worked at the check-in desk had been committed to a psychiatric ward... – Indefinitely.

As I silenced my phone and reached for another slice of pizza, another crow appeared on the railing that lined my porch. He stared at me wide-eyed, then blinked a few times, and flew away.

As the sun set, I quietly shut my laptop, grabbed a book from one of the moving boxes, and cozied up on the sofa. An audible knock came from the front door, but this time I chose to ignore it.

Was this the end, or just the very beginning, I wondered?

ABOUT THE AUTHOR

Author & Oracle Jennifer Donner has been telling tales for a while. Besides writing, Jennifer enjoys talking to herself & her dead dog/BFF forever "Meatloaf," who passed away peacefully on July 17th, 2021. She's also really good at assembling lamps. Jennifer enjoys hiking before sunrise, dancing, swimming, reading, donating to animal sanctuaries, playing a friendly game of cat & mouse with her local sheriff's department, and rescuing animals to give to her parents.

Jennifer does not enjoy small spaces, heights, large crowds, hairdryers, or the drive-through car wash.

For more book releases and stuff - follow her on IG at @stuffwithjennifer on TikTok @ stuffwithjennifer

Check out her haunted blog www.thefoodphantom.com (it's free!)

If you would like to correspond via email or be alerted when a new book is released - email her at iwritethings1154@gmail.com (please no pen pals).

PO Box 1271

Greenville, SC 29602

www.ingramcontent.com/pod-product-compliance
Lightning Source LLC
Chambersburg PA
CBHW020742130626
46554CB00006B/2110